Written by Danielle Elison Webb
Illustrated by Ignacio Guerrero

Rencher Girls-
Don't be afraid to try new things. You never know what you might discover! :)
♡, Danielle Elison Webb

www.broomstickpress.com

If your heart had a glitch,

could you ever love a witch?

Could you ever delight in the fright of midnight?

Would it be a trick or treat?
How could she possibly be sweet?

Could you ever focus,
despite her hocus pocus?

Do you think that her spell could really treat you well?

Is there something in her potion that causes such emotion?

The question is, could you ever love a witch?

Would riding on her broomstick
make you feel too sick?

Maybe the full moon would make you swoon!

You just might choose to like
her pointy shoes

and her crooked black hat and
her green-eyed cat.

But could you love all the things
that she can do with bat wings?

Maybe if the stars aligned, you
could change your mind!

You know, your heart could switch.
You might really love a witch!

Do you ever wonder what you might discover?

I've got a question for you.

The question is,

could you ever love a witch?

For my little wizard and three adorable witches
– D.E.W.

First Edition 2014
Broomstick Press

ISBN: 978-0-9907384-1-1 (hardcover)
978-0-9907384-2-8 (paperback)
978-0-9907384-0-4 (eBook)
Library of Congress Control Number: 2014915787

Printed in China

Based on the original song

"Could You Ever Love a Witch?"

Music by Bret Scherer & Kimberly Woodland
Words by Danielle Elison Webb

2013 Grand Prize Winner, Children's Category
The International John Lennon Songwriting Contest

To access your free digital download of the song, visit
http://www.broomstickpress.com/music

and enter promotional download code at checkout:

LOVEAWITCH